THE BUSY BEAVER

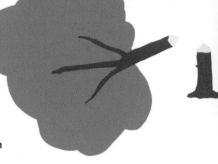

To John, Chris and Jeremy

First paperback edition 2016

Text and illustrations © 2011 Nicholas Oldland

Kids Can Press gratefully acknowledges the financial support of the Government of
Ontario, through the Ontario Media Development Corporation; the Ontario Arts Council;
the Canada Council for the Arts; and the Government of Canada, through the CBF,
for our publishing activity.

Published in Canada and the U.S. by Kids Can Press Ltd.
25 Dockside Drive, Toronto, ON M5A 0B5

Kids Can Press is a Corus Entertainment Inc. company

www.kidscanpress.com

The artwork in this book was rendered in Photoshop.
The text is set in Animated Gothic and Handysans.

Edited by Yvette Ghione
Designed by Marie Bartholomew and Julia Naimska

Printed and bound in Malaysia in 3/2018 by Tien Wah Press (Pte.) Ltd.

CM 11 20 19 18 17 16 15 14 13 12 11 10 9
CM PA 16 0 9 8 7 6 5 4 3

Library and Archives Canada Cataloguing in Publication

Oldland, Nicholas, 1972–
The busy beaver / Nicholas Oldland.

(Life in the wild)
For ages 3–7.
ISBN 978-1-55453-749-5 (bound)   ISBN 978-1-55453-790-7 (paperback)

I. Beavers — Juvenile fiction. I. Title. II. Series: Oldland, Nicholas, 1972–. Life in the wild.

PS8629.L46B88 2011   jC813'.6   C2011-901072-0

FSC
www.fsc.org
MIX
Paper from
responsible sources
FSC® C012700

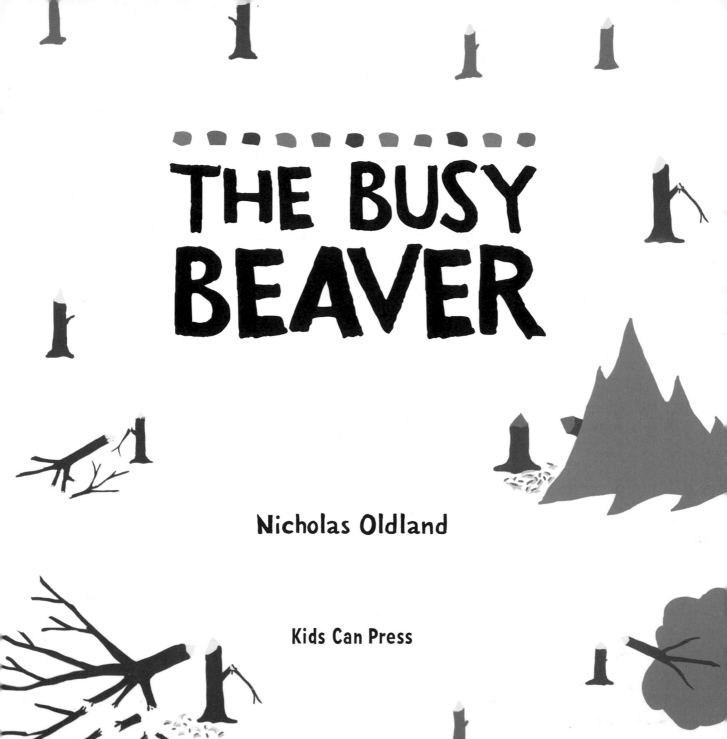

THE BUSY BEAVER

Nicholas Oldland

Kids Can Press

There once was a beaver who was so busy
that he didn't always think things through.

This beaver's carelessness was becoming a problem. His dams leaked, and he always made a mess of the forest — he left trees half-chewed, and, worse, he felled more than he needed.

Perhaps worst of all, the beaver went about his work with so little thought that a tree landed right on top of a bear.

And once he even chewed a moose's leg thinking it was a tree.

The beaver was just that careless.

It was only a matter of time before something went terribly wrong.

CRACK!

Sure enough, one day the beaver was so busy chewing on a tree that he failed to notice it was falling in his direction.

The beaver woke up in the hospital with a bent tail, two broken limbs, three cracked ribs, four big bruises, five sprained fingers, six twisted toes, seven little cuts, eight stinging scratches, nine sore muscles and ten nasty slivers.

He had spent his entire life chewing, swimming and building. He had never sat still for a second. Now he could barely even scratch his nose.

At first all the beaver could
do was stare at the ceiling.

But little by little,
he began to heal.

With lots of rest, he
regained his strength.

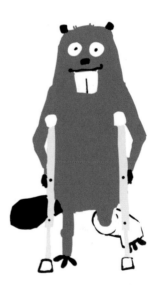

And before too long,
he was trying out a
pair of crutches.

Eventually the beaver was able to hobble over to the window. This was the first time he noticed his leaky dam, the mess of trees he had left half-chewed, his friends' bandages and a family of homeless birds.

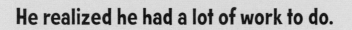

He realized he had a lot of work to do.

The next day, the beaver embarked on a rigorous rehabilitation program.

He got back on his feet ...

Did lots of yoga ...

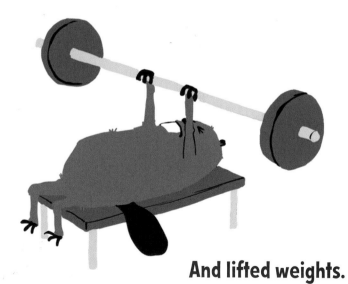

And lifted weights.

While he was at it, the beaver caught up on some important reading ...

And practiced saying "I'm sorry."

Soon enough he was ready to go home.

The beaver's friends were a little worried about his return to the forest. But despite their concerns, the beaver went straight to work.

HI, GUYS!

Before the beaver started his first project, he did a full tree inspection ...

Checked to see if there were any animals in harm's way ...

And carried a frightened caterpillar to safety.

Then the beaver went ahead and built the family of homeless birds a new nest.

Next the beaver apologized to his friends for being careless and causing so much damage.

To show that he meant it, he made the bear a vase for his den.

And he built a canoe for the moose.

The beaver's final task was to clean up the mess he had made in the forest.

He hauled off the trees he had left half-chewed ...

Used the broken branches to fix his leaky dam ...

And planted saplings to replace the trees he had felled.

With the forest back in order, everyone
was happier, including the beaver.

His work done, the beaver got to thinking about what he might do next. He came up with lots of ideas as he got ready for bed that night.

Maybe he would take a course on dam building ...

Or start a band and go on tour ...

Or take more naps. The beaver liked this idea best.

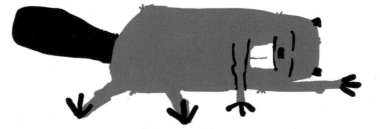

Being busy doing good work was exhausting. With a yawn, the beaver laid his head down on a soft bed of leaves and fell right to sleep.

All that was left for the beaver to do was dream.